5

‖‖‖‖‖‖‖‖‖‖‖‖‖‖‖‖‖‖‖‖
☞ **W9-BGR-469**

DATE DUE

FEB 2 6 1996			

J. CAR   96-1

JAKY OR DODO

St. Mary School
829 W. Madison St.
Alexandria, IN 46001

DEMCO

JAKY OR DODO?

ST. MARY SCHOOL
LIBRARY

JAKY OR DODO?

Natalie Savage Carlson

Pictures by Gail Owens

Charles Scribner's Sons · New York

ST. MARY SCHOOL
LIBRARY

J
Carlson

Copyright © 1978 Natalie Savage Carlson

Library of Congress Cataloging in Publication Data
Carlson, Natalie Savage.
  Jaky or Dodo?
  SUMMARY: A Parisian mongrel successfully leads a
double life until both of his "owners" enter him in the
same dog show.
  1. Dogs—Legends and stories.   [1. Dogs—Fiction.
2. Paris—Fiction]   I. Owens, Gail.   II. Title.
PZ10.3.C2Jak   [E]   77-21241
ISBN 0-684-15340-8

This book published simultaneously in the
United States of America and in Canada—
Copyright under the Berne Convention

All rights reserved. No part of this book
may be reproduced in any form without the
permission of Charles Scribner's Sons.

1 3 5 7 9 11 13 15 17 19 MD/C 20 18 16 14 12 10 8 6 4 2

Printed in the United States of America

Moyer 10/7/85 3.31

For
ALTHEA ANDERSEN,
who lights the candle
for story hour at the library

110265
ST. MARY SCHOOL
LIBRARY

JAKY OR DODO?

THE hill of Montmartre rises disdainfully above the chimney pots of Paris and does not admit belonging to that French city. Its citizens feel so independent that they have their own mayor.

But even more independent than the people of Montmartre was a little brown and white dog who wore no collar. He was a *corniaud*, which is a fancy French word for a mongrel.

One late afternoon, he was hurrying down the steep, narrow streets, his long beard almost sweeping

them. His wavy sideburns streamed in the breeze.
But he didn't go in a straight path. He took a leisurely
route. Here to there, back and forth, *ici* to *là*, *là* to
ici. He paused to sniff a post marked *Barré*; this meant
that the alley beyond was barred to automobiles—
though not to him. He broke up a romance between
two pigeons and jumped over a bicycle lying on the
sidewalk.

Lower and lower he zigzagged and sniffed until
the great church of Sacré Coeur on the hill looked no
bigger than an ice cream cone. The streets were silent
and almost empty.

At last the little dog turned into an alleyway
scarcely wide enough for two wheelbarrows to pass.
He picked up speed as he sprinted for the open gate-
way at the end.

A boy was waiting to meet him, a sturdy boy with
tangled black bangs and two front teeth missing.

"Jaky, where have you been?" he demanded.
"Why do you stay away so much? Don't you know
that Mémère has given us permission to go all the
way to the park today?"

Jaky crawled on his stomach toward the boy.
"*Ouaf, ouaf,*" he apologized.

They went toward the little glassed-in booth near

the gate. The boy's grandmother, Madame Duval, was concierge of the rooming house. That means she was manager, janitor, and woman of all work and little pay.

She stopped sorting the tenants' mail long enough to frown at the dog.

"So he is back again," she declared. "Someday he will not return. A *corniaud* is not to be trusted, Pierre. A tramp dog! That's all your Jaky is."

"He is not a tramp," retorted Pierre. "He wants to be free sometimes—just like me out of school this summer. Remember how he followed me home so willingly? He wasn't wearing a collar, so I knew he didn't belong to anyone. But he's my dog now. Can't we buy him a collar and license?"

His grandmother shook an envelope at him. "When I buy a collar and license for a dog," she stated, "it will be for a purebred Pomeranian like so many other concierges have. A purebred dog has elegance."

Pierre had heard about this Pomeranian so many times that he turned a deaf ear to his grandmother's words. If Maman and Papa were still alive, they would love this dog as much as he. *They* would buy Jaky a collar and license.

"I suppose he is hungry," grumbled Madame Duval. "Mongrels are always hungry."

She put the envelope on top of a pile and went into the cubbyhole of a kitchen with the boy and the dog. She wanted to make sure that Pierre didn't get into the meat that was ready for their own supper. Jaky danced around her plaid carpet slippers in happy anticipation.

Madame Duval took the chipped enamel pan from the floor and spooned into it some thin broth from the simmering cabbage soup.

"The soup of our day," she told Jaky. She added some limp cabbage leaves. "And here are a few stale crusts left from breakfast. They will soften in the soup. And that end of dried sausage isn't fit for us to eat now."

She dropped the leftovers into the soup and stirred all together vigorously.

"We shall call this 'poor Pierre's *pâté*,'" she said, "like the stylish restaurants that give fancy names to food."

She set the pan on the floor, and Jaky began gulping the mixture as if he really were starving.

"He's an easy dog to feed." Pierre tried to win over his grandmother. "He eats anything we give him."

"He knows he's lucky to get anything," she retorted. "If he ever meets anyone who feeds him better
—*pouish!*—we will never see even the shadow of his
tail again."

Madame Duval returned to her glassed-in sentry
box, and Pierre cut the thinnest slice possible from
the supper meat and gave it to Jaky for dessert.

"Now for the park," he announced.

It was a long walk to the Parc des Buttes-Chaumont. It took them through wide streets and narrow ones, straight and crooked ones. And Pierre, like Jaky, liked to zigzag from *ici* to *là* so he would miss nothing.

At last they reached the great gate to the park. There were many other boys and girls entering with their parents, but Pierre didn't consider himself one of them.

"Now we're in Magic Land," he told Jaky. "I'm a knight on my way to free a beautiful princess who is captive of an evil ogre. And you're my big fierce mastiff."

He picked up a leafy branch that an older boy had discarded as unfit for a sword. "This is my magic wand against the dragons that guard her."

They climbed a rocky path that led to a tunnel through the side of a steep cliff.

"The dragon's lair," explained Pierre, waving his branch against the cavelike sides of the tunnel. He just missed striking an old gentleman who threatened with his own magic wand, a wooden cane, then hurried past.

"We dispatched that dragon," announced Pierre triumphantly.

Out of the dragon's cave and up another rocky path to a longer tunnel they climbed.

"A whole army of dragons lives here," whispered Pierre to his fierce mastiff as he bravely plunged into the dim tunnel.

The dragons turned out to be a group of little girls having an outing with a tall nun.

"*Bou-ou-ou!*" Pierre made moaning sounds in the duskiness of the tunnel. He thrashed the sides with his magic wand.

Some of the little girls squealed with fright and others ran for the exit.

"Shame on you for scaring such little ones!" scolded the nun, not realizing that her charges were really threatening dragons. But in the face of Jaky's impudent barks, even she retreated. The dragons had been conquered.

Pierre looked through a windowlike hole in the rocky wall.

"The princess!" he cried. "There she is, sailing on the lake. And look at those evil monsters guarding her!"

He lifted the dog in his arms so he, too, could view the beautiful maiden in distress.

"*Ouaf, ouaf*," barked Jaky, which meant, "They only look like a swan and a pair of ducks to me."

On up the hill struggled the victorious knight with his faithful mastiff. At the top of the path was the ogre's castle which was a little round pavilion ringed by pillars. It sat on the edge of a sheer crag.

A long-tailed magpie squawked from its dome.
Pierre shook his magic wand at the bird.

"I challenge you to fight, wicked ogre!" he
shouted.

The magpie gave a surprised squawk, then rose
on its black and white wings, trailing its long tail
over the blue lake.

"Now the princess is free," said Pierre.

So that ended the story because Pierre threw the
branch away and spent the rest of the time rolling on
the grass with Jaky.

It was quite late when they reached home after
their exciting afternoon.

"And what did you do at the park?" asked Madame Duval, checking the keys at her waist.

"Nothing much," replied Pierre. "We just went through some tunnels to the top of the cliff and saw some birds."

When night spread its own magpie wings over the hill of Montmartre, Madame Duval called to Jaky.

"Out, Jaky!" she ordered. "Your doghouse is waiting for you in the courtyard. You must be a watchdog, else why should we feed you?"

Jaky dutifully went into the little doghouse which had belonged to the Pomeranian of the former concierge. He pressed his beard between his paws and closed his eyes. He slept so soundly that even if an intruder had dared climb over the broken glass sprinkled on top of the wall, Jaky wouldn't have heard a tinkle.

But at dawn, he clearly heard the roar of the baker's little Simca car. He opened one eye and raised one ear. He listened to the creaking of the gate. He opened his other eye and raised his other ear. Then, as the baker slowly drove out, Jaky jumped up and raced for the open gate. He was through it like a moving shadow before the man had time to climb out of his car to close it.

JAKY spent the morning down in the city of Paris. He strolled the boulevards and flirted with lady poodles. He outran a dogcatcher and insulted the statue of a general.

Then it began to rain pins and needles and bayonets, so he retraced his steps to Montmartre. The gutters were flooding and waterfalls poured down the steep side streets. It was a sight to delight the street sweepers.

ST. MARY SCHOOL
LIBRARY

High on the hill, Jaky made for the door of a building whose sign proclaimed it to be the Café of the Jolly Artist.

All the tables and chairs had been moved indoors for the midday meal. The dining room was packed tight as a chestnut burr. The only artist present was a gloomy young man who never ordered more than the soup of the day. But there were plenty of businessmen dining on the specialty of the house, which happened to be chicken supreme of Bresse with truffles.

"He's here," announced Madame Berthe, the owner's wife, who sat at a desk near the door where the patrons paid their bills.

A stir rippled the red and white checked tablecloths.

The owner rushed from the kitchen with a long, dripping spoon in his hand. His ample paunch under his white chef's apron gave him something of the shape of the force-fed geese of Strasbourg which he sometimes offered on his menu. His moustache ends twitched like the wingtips of a nervous sparrow.

"Where have you been all morning, Dodo?" he sternly asked the dog, who looked like a wet mop. "And where did you spend the night? Where do you spend all your nights?"

Dodo—or was he Jaky?—made no answer. He only shook himself vigorously.

"Why do you worry about him, Monsieur Boffu?" asked the artist. "He is only a mongrel."

"Because he is my dog. Didn't I find him sitting on my doormat one morning—with no collar? Didn't I give him a name and a home? Of all the people in Montmartre, he chose me for his master."

"If he is your dog," put in Madame Berthe, "you should buy him a collar and a license tag to hang on it."

"Indeed not!" declared Monsieur. "A collar is the symbol of a dog's slavish dependence. Dodo is an independent dog of Montmartre. He even carries his tail with independence."

At this tribute, Dodo—or Jaky—went to Monsieur and gave his hand an affectionate lick. Then the man, bowing like one of his waiters, beckoned the dog to the only empty chair. Dodo jumped up on it, then looked over the room with a lordly air. Monsieur vanished into the kitchen only to return quickly with a big plate loaded with food.

"Chicken supreme of Bresse with truffles," he announced as he set the dish before Dodo. He pushed his tall chef's cap to one side and folded his arms proudly.

Summitville Community Library
Summitville, IN 46870

Dodo deigned to sniff the food, then lifted his
own truffle of a nose into the air.

"What's wrong this time?" demanded Monsieur.
"Isn't the chicken plump enough to suit you? Is it
seasoned too highly, or not enough?"

Dodo turned his head away, then jumped down
from the chair. He crawled on his stomach to Monsieur, then barked, "*Ouaf, ouaf.*"

"I think he is trying to tell you something," said
Madame Berthe, "but I don't know what it is."

"He is really fond of you," said a stout diner

110265

nearby. "He knows you are fond of him, too. A dog senses such things."

"Then why isn't he fond of my food?" asked Monsieur. "You know the old saying—'Love me, love my dog.' Well, I say to my dog, 'Love me, love my food.' "

The stout diner tried to soothe his host. "The chicken supreme is really supreme," he said, "but perhaps Dodo would prefer pressed duck."

Madame Berthe made quick change for a ten-franc note. "He was offered that only two days ago," she said, "and he refused it. The dog will starve to death."

"But he looks as well filled as the skin of a sausage," said the stout diner, who was well filled himself.

"Perhaps he prefers to make the rounds of the garbage cans," suggested the artist. "Mongrels don't like rich food. They aren't used to it."

Now Dodo was making the rounds of the table legs and human legs. He finally went to sleep under a table with the stout man's shoe for his pillow.

The rain stopped and the sun came out.

One by one, the customers left, the waiters cleared the tables, and Madame Berthe went over her accounts.

The stout patron read his newspaper, then care-

fully studied the bill. After much figuring, he decided it was correct and no one had tried to cheat him. He pulled his foot from under Dodo's head and went to the desk to pay Madame Berthe. As he walked to the door, Dodo jumped up and followed him.

"Stop!" cried Monsieur. "Don't let the dog out or he may not be back until tomorrow morning."

As the patron stood with the door half open to listen to Monsieur's command, Dodo neatly slipped through it and raced down the street.

"There he goes again," said Madame, "and he has spent less than an hour here today. Where is he going? Why doesn't he eat?"

An angry light filled Monsieur Boffu's eyes. He waved his long spoon.

"Aha!" he cried, his plump belly quivering with rage. "I have it! Some other cook is feeding him. That's where Dodo goes. To some fine restaurant down in the city. I shall follow him next time and discover where he spends his secret life. I shall challenge this chef to a duel of the pots. We shall find out who makes the best chicken supreme of Bresse with truffles."

IT was a few days before Monsieur Boffu could find
time to follow Dodo. There was always a soufflé
to raise or an aspic to set.

But one day he left the kitchen in the hands of the
headwaiter and stood in the open doorway to breathe
deeply of the fresh air.

"A fine day for adventure and solving mysteries," he declared. "Isn't that so, Dodo?" he added, because the dog had slipped beneath Monsieur's legs and was on his way down the street.

Monsieur Boffu closed the door behind him. He followed Dodo from what he considered a safe distance.

The dog didn't notice he was being followed until he stopped to sniff a weed growing from the grating around a tree. Then, from the corner of his eye, he caught sight of Monsieur.

Dodo lost interest in the weed. He turned down an alley. He began to run. Monsieur made the turn, and he began to run, too. Sometimes the dog went *là* when Monsieur was *ici*. Or Monsieur turned *là* when Dodo went *ici*. Monsieur was now huffing and puffing and blowing. He had only two legs to Dodo's four, but he was keeping the dog in sight.

All the way to Pigalle, Dodo tried to lay a false trail for Monsieur. Past the red windmill of the Moulin Rouge. Past all the theaters and cafés.

At a busy intersection, the dog glanced over his shoulder. Although the light was red, he dashed across. An autobus had to swerve to avoid hitting him. When Monsieur stepped off the curb to follow,

a policeman in a blue cape held up his asparagus club to bar the way.

"Can't you see the light is still red?" he demanded.

"But I am trying to catch my dog," protested Monsieur.

"Your dog may not cross either," said the policeman.

"But my dog is already across," explained Monsieur.

"This is very irregular. Why isn't your dog on a leash?"

But since the light had turned green, he allowed Monsieur Boffu to go on his way.

It was of little use. There were so many directions in which Dodo might have gone. Monsieur walked around a square calling, "Dodo! Dodo!"

There was no Dodo in sight. There was no Dodo anywhere; there was only Jaky, and he was nearing the end of the narrow street.

Monsieur Boffu was desolate. Why had he gone to look for noon at fourteen o'clock, as the French say of a wild goose chase? Why had he left his kitchen in the uncertain care of a headwaiter who was more interested in tips than in egg whisks and frying pans? Because of a useless *corniaud*, that was why.

He dolefully retraced his steps. He stopped for a

moment at a mushroomlike kiosk where newspapers were sold. He bought a copy of *France-Soir* to read as he slowly walked along.

Monsieur read that the present government was about to fall and that the city workers were going on strike. He bumped into another pedestrian, muttered *"Pardon,"* and opened to the sports page. A jockey had been thrown at the Longchamps races, and a soccer game at the Stade Jean-Bouin had ended in a riot. *Hélas!* Everyone had his troubles.

Then his eyes fell upon something that caused him to walk faster. It was such a cheerful something that he could hardly wait to get back to his café. He huffed and puffed and blew himself up the hill of Montmartre.

He burst into the café with the paper rolled in his hand. Madame Berthe looked up from the cashier's desk.

"The money doesn't come out right," she complained. "Somebody must have walked out without paying."

"And the mayonnaise for tonight has curdled," confessed the headwaiter.

Monsieur was impatient.

"Money and mayonnaise don't matter," he de-

clared. "Will you just listen to what is in this paper?" He unfurled it and spread the sheets across a checked tablecloth. "There is to be a show of mongrel dogs here in Montmartre next week. Besides looks, the winner will be judged on his independence of spirit."

"Then that should be Dodo," said Madame. "But what if he does win? Will that balance the money or uncurdle the mayonnaise?"

Monsieur rolled his eyes triumphantly. "But it is *what* he will win that counts." He ran his pudgy finger along the print. "A leash and a diamond-studded collar. Diamonds! They aren't to be sniffed at even by a dog."

"What else?" asked his wife.

"A complete canine wardrobe."

"That doesn't give me a new holiday dress. But I might gouge out a few diamonds from the collar and have them put into a ring."

"His portrait will be done by a famous artist right in his own studio."

"I suppose we could hang it here in the café. We might even change the name to the Café of the Handsome Corniaud."

"Then there will be a cinema contract," continued Monsieur. "Imagine our Dodo featured in all the theaters of Paris!"

"And they should let us in free."

"Last of all, he will enjoy a week's vacation at a fashionable kennel in the country."

"We are the ones who need the vacation," said Madame. "But did you find out where he went today?"

"No, because he conspired with a policeman to defeat me. But that doesn't matter now. Don't you see the most important point of this dog show? When Dodo wins, that will smoke out the villain who is feeding him. He will want a share of the glory. But I shall triumph over him."

It wasn't until the next morning that Pierre Duval found out about the dog show to be held in Montmartre.

"Carry these old newspapers to the trash can," Madame Duval ordered her grandson. "The collectors can sell them to the junk dealers for a few coins."

Pierre dutifully shouldered the bundle and carried it to the big can in the courtyard. As he squeezed the papers into it, he noticed the top sheet. Someone had folded the paper after reading the sports page. There was the picture of a riot in the stadium and right next to it an acount of the show to be held in Montmartre.

The boy's eyes grew bigger and bigger as he read about the prizes to be won. He tore off the page and ran to his grandmother.

"Mémère! Mémère!" he cried excitedly. "There is to be a big show for *corniauds,* and the handsomest will win a lot of things. I'm going to enter Jaky."

He began to read about the prizes. "If Jaky wins, he'll get a complete wardrobe. Oh, won't he be the fine dog? I bet he'll look more stylish than any Pomeranian. And a leash and a diamond-studded *collar.* I won't be asking you to buy him one anymore."

"What else?" asked Madame Duval.

"He will have his portrait painted by a famous artist."

"And what use is that? To hang in his doghouse?"

"There's a cinema contract, too. He'll probably become a great actor like Rin Tin Tin, the American dog buried in the pet cemetery here."

"Will we be paid for his work?" asked Madame. "It seems we should get some reward, too."

"It doesn't say, but he'll have a week's vacation at a fashionable kennel in the country. I bet he's never been in the country."

"Neither have you. But that will only spoil him. He will no longer be willing to eat what scraps we can provide and sleep in a secondhand doghouse."

"But think how famous he will become, Mémère. My own Jaky. I must get him right away and begin teaching him proper manners for a show."

"You will have to wait," said his grandmother. "The dog is already gone. Perhaps he thinks the show is today."

But Jaky didn't have the show on his mind at all. Nor did Dodo as he made his way to the Café of the Jolly Artist to pay his duty call on Monsieur Boffu. It was reward enough to have two affectionate masters without winning a number of things that were of no use to a *corniaud*.

PIERRE bit his nails as he looked at the hands of the clock. Most of the time he wanted them to race around, but now he had a desperate desire to hold them back.

It was the day of the *corniaud* show at Montmartre, and Jaky had vanished. He hadn't even come back the day before. Now it was time to go to the show, but still there was no sign of the dog.

"I knew we should have bought a collar for him," Pierre grieved. "The police have probably caught him. Maybe they've already taken him to the pound and put him to sleep."

"Pouf!" exclaimed Madame Duval. "That dog is too slippery and sly to be caught by anyone. He is a tramp who has found better eating somewhere else."

Pierre didn't believe this, and he didn't want to believe his own guess. He watched the clock until the hands were moving toward two.

"I think I'll go see the show anyhow," he said in a quavering voice. "Maybe Jaky has already gone to it by himself."

And this guess came closer to the truth than the other.

Monsieur Boffu had made sure that Dodo would be present for the dog show at the Place du Tertre. He had been allowed out only on a leash and wearing a collar of strong twine. After all, there is a limit to independence.

There was a great air of excitement in the Place du Tertre, a small square with many trees, bordered by small houses and cafés. Through a street opening at one side one could glimpse the dome of Sacré Coeur, looking as if it were topped with whipped cream.

The square was filled with yipping and yapping and howling and growling.

Tourists sitting at the tables under tasseled umbrellas were as noisy as the dogs.

"Look at that monster—he would be a bulldog if his nose wasn't so long."

"And the one beside him could be a basset if his ears weren't so short."

There was a spotted bull terrier and a Dalmatian without spots, a greyhound with short legs and a dachshund with long ones, an almost-spaniel and a not-quite-poodle.

Most of the dogs looked as if their masters had been given a pile of tails and ears and legs and told, "Now design an original dog. Remember that you are independent citizens of Montmartre."

The mayor was head judge. He was wearing a gray top hat, a cluster of medals, and his striped sash of office. Sitting at the table with him were the two other judges. The girl with the omelet shade of hair was the famous cinema star Souci de Simon.

The young man wearing the floppy Basque beret did television commercials for dog food.

On the very dot of two o'clock, Monsieur Boffu entered the square leading Dodo. The dog's flowing sideburns and beard had been combed in the style of the great author Victor Hugo. His coat had been brushed until it snapped with electricity. His toenails had been clipped and his ears plucked in the style of the purebred show dog. But his fluffy tail was carried in his own style.

A gasp of admiration went up from the spectators.

"He looks like a professor from the Sorbonne. So scholarly!"

"No, more like a deputy of the National Assembly. He has that air."

"And he carries his tail with such independence."

Monsieur Boffu beamed and saluted as if they were talking about him. Dodo strutted proudly at such attention. But the other dog owners frowned at him.

First came the parade around the square. Even the windows of the buildings seemed to stare at the remarkable sight. Café loungers rose to their feet and pushed toward the curb.

Suddenly a shrill voice rose above all the others.

"Jaky! Jaky! There you are!" It was the voice of
Pierre Duval.

The boy pushed his way through the crowd
toward Monsieur Boffu.

"My dog!" he panted. "That's my dog, Monsieur."

Monsieur Boffu was affronted. He reddened to
the very whites of his eyes.

"Your dog!" he exclaimed. "I don't even know
your dog. I have never seen him."

But Dodo—or Jaky—was whining and pulling at his makeshift leash to get to Pierre.

"*Ouaf! Ouaf!*" he apologized, which meant, "It has all been a horrible mistake."

Pierre fell to his knees and cuddled the dog. "He's my Jaky. He didn't come home last night, and I thought something had happened to him."

Monsieur Boffu's moustache ends quivered. "He is my Dodo, and he was home with me all night."

Commotion arose. It shook the tassels of the umbrellas. The other dog owners and their dogs growled at the interruption.

The mayor hurried over. "What is all this arguing about?" he demanded.

Monsieur was grinding his teeth with rage. "This street urchin claims my dog is his," he declared. "But would he answer to the name of Dodo if he was really Jaky? It is the boy who is an imposter. He made me believe that he was a rival cook."

"But he *is* my Jaky," persisted Pierre. "See? He even knows me." Jaky was licking Pierre's hand— but he soon turned around and began whining at Monsieur Boffu. He couldn't make up his mind to whom he belonged. The problem had never arisen before. He pittered his forepaws at Pierre, then pat-

tered them at Monsieur. He finally decided on Pierre and tried to climb his bare legs.

Witnesses quickly came forward.

"He is Monsieur Boffu's dog. Every day I see him at the café."

"And Monsieur feeds him." Which was an exaggeration.

Only the gloomy artist differed. "He is a *corniaud*, so he belongs only to himself."

No one paid any attention to the artist.

The mayor made his decision. "The dog seems to be the property of Monsieur Boffu. So run along, my little one. You are holding up the show."

Pierre blindly fought his way back through the crowd. They must be right. He had found Jaky in the streets. He had never thought that a dog without a collar belonged to anyone.

The dogs were lined up on the cobblestones while the judges went from one to another. They consulted together. At last the mayor raised his hand over Dodo.

"This dog is the handsomest," he declared, "and he truly shows an independent spirit."

The owner of the almost-spaniel shouted, "Unfair! Unfair! My dog is the best."

As he angrily advanced upon the mayor, the man with the not-quite-poodle blocked his way.

"Your dog is the worst," he declared. "My Zizi is the best."

When they were ready to come to blows, some men in the crowd separated them, although one was nipped on the ankle by Zizi.

Finally everything settled down and the mayor made his speech.

"A *corniaud* may be a dog without race," he ended, "but he has the virtues of many races. A purebred dog's ancestors are all alike. If such a dog could live in a castle with portraits of them on the walls, he couldn't even tell his grandfather from his great-aunt. But a mongrel—ah! There is the difference. His family portraits might differ as greatly as pictures hanging in the Louvre."

Dodo was lifted upon a table, and the mayor fastened a red collar studded with shiny stones around his neck. He snapped a red leather leash to it. He congratulated Monsieur Boffu and kissed him on each cheek.

"*Ouaf! Ouaf!*" barked Dodo, meaning "*I'm* the one you should kiss." Then he anxiously looked around for Pierre, but the boy was gone.

NEXT day Monsieur Boffu took Dodo to the Élégant Toutou shop on the Champs Élysées to be outfitted with the wardrobe he had won. Madame Berthe went with them because every Frenchwoman is interested in clothes—even those for a dog.

The salesgirl in charge of the doggy shop welcomed them warmly. She patted Dodo's head and plucked at his wavy beard. She called him her "dearest little *toutou*" and tweaked his tail.

It was easy to see that Dodo enjoyed this attention. But he didn't enjoy what followed.

He was set on a slippery glass table and measured from nose to tip of tail. Then the girl fluttered around like a pigeon, picking out styles she thought would be most becoming to him.

"This turtleneck sweater is just right," she cooed, as she pulled a red knit over his head and forepaws.

"It does match his leash," agreed Madame Berthe, "but isn't it too tight around the neck? One can't see his diamond collar."

The girl found another of the same color. "This is known as the 'jewel neckline.' *Voilà!* Doesn't he look divine? And now for the coat."

She opened a drawer and pulled out several.

"That mink would suit him," said Madame quickly. "There really isn't anything as elegant as fur."

The girl hesitated. Then she fastened the fur around Dodo's own. He sniffed at it, and if he thought it smelled more like rabbit than mink, he gave no sign.

"The hat's next," said the girl. "We must be very careful. A hat can make or break the whole costume."

"What about that sailor cap?" suggested Madame Berthe. "I've always had a weakness for sailors."

Monsieur Boffu was jealous. "Then why did you settle for a chef's cap?"

The salesgirl had already set the white sailor cap with its red pompon between Dodo's ears. She tilted it saucily over one eye.

"Oh, the dear little sailor!" exclaimed Madame, clasping her hands together.

"But perhaps you will be walking him in the rain sometimes," continued the girl. "He must have a

rain cape. Here's one that is very high style, and it will show the mink coat underneath. This is called our gendarme model."

She draped a fan-shaped plastic cape over Dodo's back. "And rain booties, naturally, so his precious little paws won't get muddy."

She carefully lifted one paw after another. "*Un, deux, trois, quatre,*" she counted. "Perhaps a bow for his tail. I would suggest that a poodle wear it over the forehead. But our *toutou* carries his tail with such style, that is where it should be placed."

She tied a big bow of red satin ribbon on Dodo's tail. Then she jumped back and beamed at him. "A true fashion plate! A gay dog of the boulevards!"

Madame had noticed the mirror across the aisle.

"Let him see himself," she suggested. "He will be so proud."

Monsieur Boffu lifted Dodo from the table to the mirror, as gingerly as if he were handling the most delicate soufflé.

Dodo stared at the dog in the mirror. He didn't like his foppish looks.

"*Ouaf! Ouaf!*" he barked, which meant "Sissy, sissy!"

The dog in the mirror was barking back at him scornfully.

The hair on Dodo's neck rose above the jewel neckline as he growled, *"Grau, grau!"* meaning "I challenge you to a duel."

Now the dog was growling back at him. Dodo sprang at him, ready to tear the elegant frippery from his enemy's back. The other dog leaped for

Dodo at the same time. But their noses only bumped glass.

Dodo crouched and growled again, which meant, "If I ever catch you out of that glass cage, I'll tear you to pieces."

Everyone in the shop was laughing. Dodo felt so ashamed that he hid the satin bow on his tail between his hind legs. He was glad to leave the shop where they kept dogs in glass cages.

That night Monsieur Boffu led Dodo to the empty room where he was now kept at night. He stacked the stylish wardrobe on the sofa.

"So you can admire your winnings," he told Dodo.

As soon as Monsieur's footsteps were gone, Dodo leaped upon the sofa. He busied himself pulling his wardrobe apart. He chewed the mink coat and

gnawed on the plastic rain cape. He clawed the sweater and put tooth marks in the rain booties. He tore the red ribbon to shreds. Then he peacefully went to sleep on the pile. He had put an end to that foppish dog.

Next morning, Madame Berthe was heartbroken at what had happened to the prize wardrobe.

But Monsieur didn't care. "After all, he is an independent dog of Montmartre," he declared. "If he wants to go around without any clothes on, that is his business. And the portrait will be more artistic if he is wearing none."

It turned out that the artist's studio wasn't in Montmartre. It was on the Pont des Arts, a bridge that spanned the Seine River down in Paris.

And it was no private studio. A number of young artists who hoped to be famous someday were sharing it. Their canvas was the pavement of the bridge—which was open only to pedestrians—and instead of oils they used colored chalks.

Dodo sniffed with interest at the very modern picture of a girl with one eye, two noses, and no chin. He nosed the chalked circles in which those who enjoyed the pictures were expected to drop coins.

"My, what a crowd!" noted Madame Berthe.

"It must have been well advertised in the papers," explained her husband, trying to restrain Dodo with tugs of the leash because the dog wanted to be patted by everyone standing along the fencing of the bridge. Or did he see someone he knew?

"Don't step on Napoleon!" warned a crouching artist who had just finished his portrait of the great man.

Monsieur Boffu guided Dodo around Napoleon's hat toward the side of the bridge where the mayor was waiting with his official party. The café owner raised his heavy eyebrows at the sight of the artist who was to portray Dodo. It was the gloomy young man who took soup in his café.

The artist looked even gloomier than ever. It was bad enough to be an unappreciated genius without having to make a portrait of a mongrel dog. But a *centime* was a *centime,* and enough of them dropped into his own chalked circle would pay for tomorrow's soup.

"How do you want him?" he asked Monsieur. "Full face or profile?"

"Just be sure to get his tail into the portrait," replied Monsieur. "It has such an air of independence."

The gloomy artist squatted on the pavement and

made a few swift strokes with a piece of brown chalk. But Dodo was not a very helpful subject. First he turned his full face, then his profile to the artist. He was restless. He seemed to be looking for someone in the crowd.

"If he can't hold a position longer than that, I can't catch his likeness," complained the artist.

Madame tried to hold Dodo's head still while Monsieur tried to hold his tail high. Dodo only strained and struggled and barked.

The artist angrily threw his chalk across the pavement.

"It is impossible to sketch an eel," he declared. "I refuse to make his portrait. I prefer to go hungry tomorrow."

Then a high, piping voice came from the crowd. "Down, Jaky! Sit, Jaky!"

It was Pierre. He had read about the event in the paper. He had come to watch, even if Jaky no longer was his—no longer even Jaky. He had meant to remain hidden in the crowd, but now the dog's behavior might spoil everything.

He ran to Jaky.

"Kidnapper of dogs!" cried Monsieur Boffu. "What are you doing here? It was officially ruled that Dodo belongs to me."

"I know that, Monsieur," agreed Pierre, "but I think I can make him sit still while his picture is colored. Then I'll go away."

Dodo—or Jaky—deliriously greeted Pierre for at least five minutes while the artist looked gloomier and gloomier.

"That's enough, Jaky," Pierre finally said sternly. He pushed him down on his haunches. "Sit! Sit like a good dog."

The dog obeyed. Sometimes an ear twitched and he had to blink his eyes, but otherwise he didn't move a muscle.

The artist retrieved the flung chalk. He worked quickly with more or less help offered by the crowd.

"That ear is off balance."

"Not much of the tail shows."

"You haven't caught the expression of the eyes."

The artist stubbornly did the portrait his own way because he had Montmartre independence. He gave a final touch to the diamond-studded collar, then stood up and bowed. The crowd shouted "Bravo" and a shower of coins fell into the circle.

What was even better, a well-dressed elderly man with a gold-headed cane made his way to the artist.

"A true work of art!" he exclaimed. "That expression in the eyes looks so much like my wife's when she is wistful. You must paint her portrait for me, young man."

"Here on the pavement?" asked the artist without much interest.

"Indeed not! On canvas. In my own home."

He handed the artist his card.

As he pocketed the coins from the circle, the young man no longer looked gloomy. He actually looked jolly.

Slowly the crowd left, some for the right bank of the river and others for the left. The bridge was empty except for a few less fortunate artists finishing chalk pictures and a little boy with tangled black bangs and two front teeth missing.

Pierre squatted by Jaky's picture. He petted the dog's likeness until his hands were dusty with chalk. Then he rose, walked blindly across Napoleon's nose, and went home.

Monsieur Boffu let all his customers know about Dodo's approaching debut in motion pictures.

"In just what film will he star?" asked one.

"Probably *A Dog of Flanders* or a *Lassie* picture."

"Or they may plan to film the life story of Barney, that heroic dog that saved the lives of forty people in the Alps," added Madame Berthe.

"Barney was a Saint Bernard," disputed the artist,

who was now happily eating a full-course dinner.

"They change things in the cinema," Madame reminded him.

Monsieur sighed. "But I don't see how he keeps alive. He only eats an occasional scrap that falls on the floor."

"Perhaps he is on a diet," suggested the stout man, who should have been on one himself. "Cinema stars must watch their figures."

Again Monsieur closed his café for the afternoon and went to the address which he had been given. He was accompanied by Madame Berthe—and Dodo, of course.

"I still regret that he destroyed his beautiful wardrobe," wailed Madame. "So far his prizes have turned out badly. The very idea of making his portrait on the floor of a bridge for everyone to walk over and the street sweepers to wash away! But the greatest disappointment of all was when that jeweler told me the diamonds in his collar are only glass."

"But when he acts in the cinema today," Monsieur consoled her, "his portrait will be all over France—all over the whole world. Perhaps you will get your diamonds yet."

They were surprised to find that the address was

that of an *épicerie*, a grocery store, on a side street instead of in a film company's studio. But there were cameras set up and lights that were brighter than daylight.

Again a curious crowd had gathered. It looked as if everyone and his Uncle Charlot had come to watch the filming.

A man in a floppy Basque beret stepped out to meet Monsieur Boffu. Monsieur recognized him as one of the judges of the dog show. They shook hands while Dodo accepted the pats of the people nearby. He expectantly sniffed each hand.

"We will start immediately now that our star has arrived," said the man. "Bring out the wagon."

The door of the store opened and a man in a gray apron pulled out a little red wagon piled with cans. The cans were labeled "Toutou Yum Yum, your dog's complete dinner." There was a picture of a dog below, but it bore no resemblance to Dodo.

The man in the beret was the director. He ordered, "Now you will take the dog inside the store, Monsieur Boffu. When I give the signal, you will emerge with the dog leading. At sight of the wagon, he will pull the leash from your hand and race for the cans of Toutou Yum Yum."

Monsieur was doubtful. "How do you know he will do that?" he asked.

The director flapped the piece of paper in his hand. "Because the script says so." He read, "Dog sees wagon filled with Toutou Yum Yum. His eyes brighten. His tail wags. He begins to drool, then breaks away from his master and races to wagon."

"I don't think Dodo will do it," persisted Monsieur.

The director shook the piece of paper. "The script says he will."

Monsieur shrugged helplessly. He led Dodo inside the store and waited while the lights were adjusted again and one camera moved to a better position.

On signal he opened the door and pulled Dodo out. The dog had no interest in the wagonload of Toutou Yum Yum. He strained at the leash to go in another direction. He was more interested in someone in the crowd.

"No, no!" shouted the director. "He is going the wrong way. The dog food is over there."

Monsieur was ruffled. "He goes his own way because he is an independent dog of Montmartre."

The director was baffled. "Perhaps we should

have someone pull the wagon to him, although I
don't know how the script writer will like that."

A boy with tangled black bangs and two teeth
missing eagerly sprang from the crowd.

"I'll pull the wagon, Monsieur," he offered.
"Jaky will come to me."

Monsieur Boffu was furious. "Imposter!" he
shouted. "You have no right to do anything more
with my dog."

"Let the boy try," commanded the director. Head
of a donkey! The man was worse than his dog.

So Monsieur took Dodo inside again and Pierre picked up the handle of the red wagon. When the door was opened for action, Dodo's eyes brightened and he wagged his tail. He jerked the leash loose from Monsieur. He sprang at Pierre, barking and licking. He still had no interest in Toutou Yum Yum.

"Show him a can, boy!" shouted the director. "Quickly!"

Pierre grabbed a can from the pile and held it to Dodo. The dog was so happy to be with his young master again that he even licked the can.

"Perfect!" cried the director. "A dramatic performance!"

But Monsieur Boffu wasn't satisfied with the scene at all. "This little urchin has a bigger role than mine," he complained. "I am the owner of the dog so I should be given more of a part."

The director had a solution. "We will continue the action," he said. "You will walk over to the boy and pat him on the head. Then you, too, will hold up a can of Toutou Yum Yum."

Monsieur had to agree, although the very idea of patting that annoying little urchin's head revolted him. But an actor must make sacrifices for his art.

He gave Pierre a few pats that were more like

slaps, then held up a can of the dog food. He wished he could give the boy a pounding on the head with it.

"Just what will the name of this picture be?" he asked the director.

The man in the beret answered, "It has no name because it's only a television commercial."

THERE was an air of gloom about Monsieur
Boffu's café. Only the artist eating his seven-
course dinner looked jolly.

Dodo was sprawled on the floor with his leash
fastened to a table leg. He didn't look like the handsomest *corniaud* in Montmartre.

"Somehow he has lost his spirit," remarked Madame Berthe. "He is growing so thin."

The artist had his own independent idea of what

was wrong with Dodo. "You have tried to make a purebred dog out of a mongrel," he said.

Now everyone listened with respect to the artist, who had been commissioned to paint the Duchesse de Brie. Many nodded, but not Madame Berthe.

"It is a good thing that he will be taking his vacation at that fashionable kennel tomorrow," she said. "It will be a tonic for him."

"Quite right, my pretty cabbage," agreed Monsieur. "The country air will do wonders. He will return as the old Dodo with his old air of independence."

Dodo only gazed at them sadly and tried to wag his limp tail.

A special little doggie van came to get him, driven by a stringbean of a fellow in a blue uniform.

Dodo didn't want to go with him. The van looked like that of the dogcatcher which he had so far eluded. He dug his nails between the cobblestones and growled. That bit of independence was left to him.

"You mean this dog was chosen the handsomest *corniaud* in Montmartre?" asked the thin fellow in uniform. Like the owners of the almost-spaniel and the not-quite-poodle, he thought the contest must have been unfair.

Monsieur Boffu finally pulled Dodo from the cobblestones and put him in the back of the van. It drove away slowly, leaving Monsieur with tears in his eyes and a burned sauce on his stove.

The van bumped along toward the suburbs, passing grim factories and long blocks of workmen's housing. It soon reached open country where golden fields of ripening wheat were splashed with pools of blue cornflowers. It passed ruined castles and chugged through quaint villages. But Dodo couldn't see any of this because he was shut up inside.

A fresh breeze carried the smell of green fields and wildflowers through the trees. But Dodo could smell only the disinfectant that had been used to clean the van.

At the Kennel of Louis XIV—so called, although it was run by a Madame Hache rather than the former king of France—Madame herself came out to meet them. With her wooden outdoor shoes and big hands, she could have passed for an aging milkmaid as well as for a concierge of dogs.

"Is this the dog?" she asked as she helped Dodo out. "He looks as if he came from the Flea Market."

"It's the dog they gave me," said the fellow, who was her son, Hubert. "But I think there has been some trickery."

Madame unlocked the gate that led to the kennel with its yard and barking tenants.

"The apartment de luxe has been reserved for you," she told Dodo, hoping this would revive his spirits. "It has its own private runway in which you may exercise at will without mixing with the other dogs."

When Madame left, Dodo pointed his nose to the

dainty little chandelier hanging from the ceiling and
howled mournfully. *"Hurle, hurle, hurle!"* He surely
thought that he was in the dog pound at last.

It was three days later that Monsieur Boffu had a
phone call from Madame Hache.

"Monsieur, I have bad news for you. Your dog is
pining away at being parted from you. He howls day

and night. He won't eat. He is even making the other dogs sad. They are going around with their noses and tails to the ground. It will give Louis XIV a bad name. I am returning Dodo to you. My son is already on the way with him."

Monsieur sighed as he hung up the receiver. He sighed as he told his wife about it. He sighed as he pounded the beefsteak.

"I shall take him to the veterinarian," he decided. "It is my last resort."

Monsieur Boffu sat in Dr. Munifre's waiting room with Dodo stretched over his knees. He was in like company. There were others waiting with their ailing loved ones.

A woman with a Pekingese kept assuring her pet that the doctor wouldn't hurt him at all.

The man with the shaggy eyebrows explained to the woman with the spaniel that his shaggy-browed Airedale had insomnia. "She frisks about all night and sleeps all day. So now I have insomnia, too."

A man still wearing his butcher's apron kept a tight leash on his bulldog who wanted to fight the boxer across the way.

And the woman gripping a striped cat sat off by herself, giving a cold eye to the dog lovers.

At last Monsieur Boffu's name was called. He hurried into the inner office carrying Dodo in his arms.

"What is wrong with your dog?" asked Dr. Munifre.

"If I knew, I wouldn't be here," said Monsieur. "He refuses to eat, and you can see that he has lost all desire to live."

Dr. Munifre set Dodo on a high table. He took his temperature. He pushed a flat wooden stick down his throat. He peered into his ears. He listened to his heart.

"There is nothing physically wrong with your dog," he finally decided. "It is a sickness of the spirit. Have you done anything to make him unhappy?"

Monsieur Boffu indignantly denied this.

"Perhaps the food you are giving him is of poor quality and he feels slighted."

Monsieur was even more indignant. "He is offered the same food as the customers in my café."

The doctor shrugged. "It may still be of poor quality."

Monsieur Boffu angrily scooped Dodo from the table. "Your medical advice may be of poor quality," he retorted.

· 73 ·

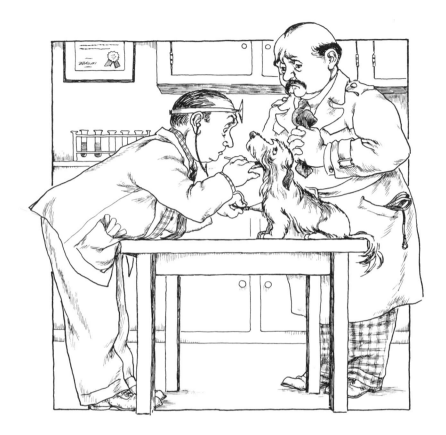

But once outside the veterinarian's office, Monsieur realized that he would have to face an unpleasant fact at last. It was one he had tried to keep hidden from himself.

Dodo was lonesome for that urchin of a boy.

And how did he know that the boy hadn't owned the dog first? He himself had only found Dodo lying on his doormat without a collar. Perhaps he really was Jaky.

Monsieur Boffu knew that he was called upon to make a great sacrifice. Was he capable of it?

When they were halfway back to the Café of the Jolly Artist, Monsieur found that he had more courage than he had supposed. He squared his shoulders.

"You lead the way wherever you want to go," he told the dog, "because I don't know where it is."

Dodo led Monsieur past the flights of stairs that ascended to the church of Sacré Coeur. He led him through a group of artists in the middle of a narrow street, all painting the same view of the church. He led him to the busy street crossing where the light was now green. He knew exactly where he was going.

As he pattered along, Dodo slowly changed before Monsieur's very eyes. His head was rising higher and higher. His sideburns and beard fluffed in the breeze. His eyes brightened. His tail slowly rose.

By the time they reached the gate at the end of the narrow street, Dodo was the handsomest mongrel again. He carried his tail with independence.

When Madame Duval answered the ringing of

the gate bell, she was surprised to see Jaky—a new Jaky with red leash and glass-studded collar, although a much thinner Jaky.

She called to her grandson. "Can you believe it, Pierre? Jaky has come back to visit you. He looks prosperous."

Pierre was more surprised than his grandmother. He tried to be polite to Monsieur Boffu even though he didn't know the reason for the visit. Perhaps Monsieur had come to threaten him with arrest if he ever approached Jaky again.

Jaky—no longer Dodo—had no hesitation. He sprang into Pierre's arms. He licked his face. He barked "*Ouaf, ouaf,*" which meant "I nearly died of being separated from you."

Monsieur Boffu pulled a handkerchief as big as one of his napkins from his pocket. He honked his nose with deep feeling.

"The dog is really Jaky," he said. "He belongs to you."

It took a few moments for Pierre to understand.

His grandmother understood first. "And do the collar and leash go with him? They do make him look as important as a purebred Pomeranian."

Meanwhile Pierre was struggling with his own

· 76 ·

conscience. Monsieur Boffu was so generous to give Jaky back to him. Generosity, although a virtue, is as catching as measles. It was only natural that Pierre should catch some of Monsieur's.

"Why can't we share Jaky, Monsieur?" he asked, surprised to hear the offer coming from his own lips. "Like we have done before. I think that is the way he would like it."

Monsieur welcomed the chance to save half a dog. "Agreed!" he declared.

Madame Duval had her interest in the proposition. "Since you own half of Jaky," she suggested, "perhaps it should be the front half so you can feed his mouth."

"But what would I do with just a tail?" asked Pierre.

"It is the tail that shows a dog's feelings," his grandmother reminded him. "I myself believe that a dog's heart is directly connected with his tail."

Still Pierre wasn't satisfied. "Why can't we divide him down the middle and each own a side?" he suggested.

"Why not?" asked Monsieur. "The boy has the wisdom of a Solomon, Madame."

All three were satisfied, although Madame had another consideration.

"But you will feed your front half of the dog's mouth, won't you?" she persisted to Monsieur.

Monsieur Boffu reddened with shame. "Madame," he confessed, "I cook the best food in Montmartre, but the dog will not eat it."

Pierre had an explanation. "Perhaps it isn't your food," he said. "Maybe you don't know the proper manner in which to serve a *corniaud*. I will bring Jaky to your café tomorrow and teach you how."

Monsieur Boffu was even more ashamed. He had once looked forward to a great cooking contest with another fine chef. And how had it all ended? A mere boy was coming to his café to teach him how to feed a dog. It was the supreme humiliation.

Ah, well, he thought to himself, it takes nobility of character to be humble, and I have always had that.

"Yes," he agreed. "You must bring Jaky to my café tomorrow and give me a lesson in the fine art of feeding a dog."

THE next morning Pierre decided that it might
be a good idea to take Jaky for a long walk before they went to Monsieur Boffu's café. It would
sharpen the dog's appetite.

They wandered from *ici* to *là* and from *là* to *ici*.

They went all the way down to Paris proper.
They looked at the display in a shoe store window in
which the latest footwear was set on real moss among

sprigs of real heather. But the next window had a necklace of sausages linked around a white pig's head. This was more to Jaky's interest.

"*Ouaf, ouaf!*" he barked. "I'd rather have some of those than a pair of shoes."

They watched a herd of little donkeys on their way to give rides to children in the Bois de Boulogne. The man driving them along was eating a hunk of bread.

"*Ouaf, ouaf!*" barked Jaky. "I'd rather have a bite of that bread than a ride on a donkey."

Pierre let him linger at a *boucherie* where the butcher was trimming lamb chops on a marble counter.

"*Ouaf, ouaf!* I'm starving."

Pierre decided that Jaky was in the right mood for teaching Monsieur Boffu how a dog should be fed. So they took the long walk back to Montmartre, and there was no *ici* and *là* about it.

Monsieur Boffu was impatiently waiting for them. The café was empty at that time, but Monsieur had reserved a special table for Jaky. It was set with a snow white tablecloth. Pierre looked doubtfully at the high chair and the napkin folded in the shape of a calla lily.

"Now for the lesson," said Monsieur. "Up into your chair, Dodo—I mean, Jaky."

"No, no," objected Pierre. "The first thing I must teach you is that Jaky won't eat off a table. He's used to eating on the floor."

Monsieur was disappointed.

"But we must have some elegance in the Café of the Jolly Artist," he insisted. "I shall spread the napkin on the floor."

"Not yet," said Pierre. "Jaky likes to smell the kitchen before he eats."

"Yes, yes," agreed Monsieur quickly. "That is the true test of a gourmet. Smell is as important as taste. One might say they cannot be divided."

They went back to the clean and shiny kitchen where gleaming copper pots hung from hooks and long sharp knives hung on the walls.

Monsieur pointed to a simmering pot and lifted the lid so that the fragrant odor steamed forth.

"*Ouaf, ouaf!*" Jaky pleaded for a spoonful.

Monsieur Boffu described the glories of the dishes he had prepared as he lifted lid after lid.

"For the appetizer, cold cooked vegetables emboldened by vinegar," he declaimed. "A tossed salad —the greens have been tossed through five rinsings.

For the fish course, blushing salmon from far-off Canada to be gowned in a rich egg sauce." Jaky looked ready to swoon. "Naturally the main course will be my chicken of Bresse wedded to white wine and flirting with truffles."

"What is he having for dessert?" asked Pierre, because that was his own favorite course.

"Frosty ice cream embraced by meringue and nestling in spun sugar. Lastly, fruit and cheese—saucy apples from Normandy to vie with brisk cheese from Provence."

Now that Pierre had savored the forthcoming meal himself, he began to think of Jaky.

"But, Monsieur," he objected, "you must not serve Jaky in courses. Everything must be mixed together. It is the most important thing to know when feeding a dog."

Monsieur Boffu was shocked. "A jumble of cuisine?" he asked. "In the Café of the Jolly Artist? Only in foreign countries do they eat such a mess."

"That's the way dogs prefer it," insisted Pierre.

"*Ouaf, ouaf!*" barked Jaky in agreement.

Although it went against Monsieur's finer feelings, he stirred all the food together on a large platter. He led Pierre and Jaky back to the dining

room and set the platter down on the white napkin.

Jaky almost buried his head in it. He gulped and slurped and choked from time to time. He swelled and swelled as he worked to the bottom of the platter.

"You see, Monsieur," Pierre concluded the lesson. "It is really very easy to feed a dog."

"Excellent!" exclaimed Monsieur Boffu. "But I am glad that none of my patrons are dogs. It would really lower the tone of my café. When Jaky returns tomorrow, however, I shall see that he is properly served."

Jaky gave a grand, rolling belch, then fell asleep.

He had given them both a lesson—that a mongrel returns love and loyalty even if they are offered by more than one master.

Some of NATALIE SAVAGE CARLSON's best loved books are, like *Jaky or Dodo?*, set in France, where she and her husband lived for several years. Among these are *The Family Under the Bridge* and the popular *Orphelines* books. Ms. Carlson's most recent books include *Marie Louise's Heyday* and *Runaway Marie Louise*. In 1966 she was the United States nominee for the Hans Christian Andersen International Children's Book Award in recognition of her entire body of work.

Gail Owens has illustrated more than twenty books, including *A Bedtime Story*, *Romansgrove*, and *F*T*C* Superstar*.